STICKER STORIES

AIRPLANES

Illustrated by Edward Miller

Grosset & Dunlap
An Imprint of Penguin Group (USA) Inc.

ISBN 978-0-448-41963-3   20 19 18 17

Up, up, and away!
Ever since the first flying machines were invented,
people have loved to take to the sky.

Airplanes can take you far, far away.
Where are these airplanes headed today?

Some planes can do fancy tricks in the air.
Pilots practice long and hard so that they
can put on dazzling air shows.

In big cities, planes do all sorts of things—from helping news channels report on traffic to getting people to hospitals in a hurry.

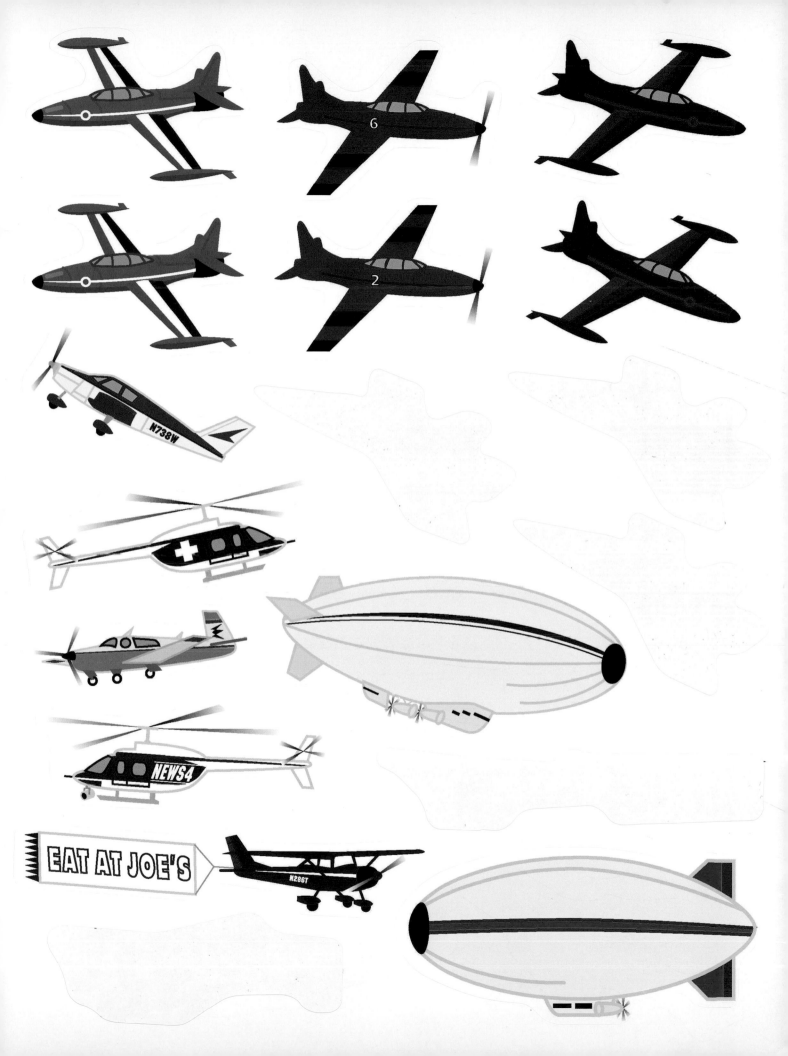

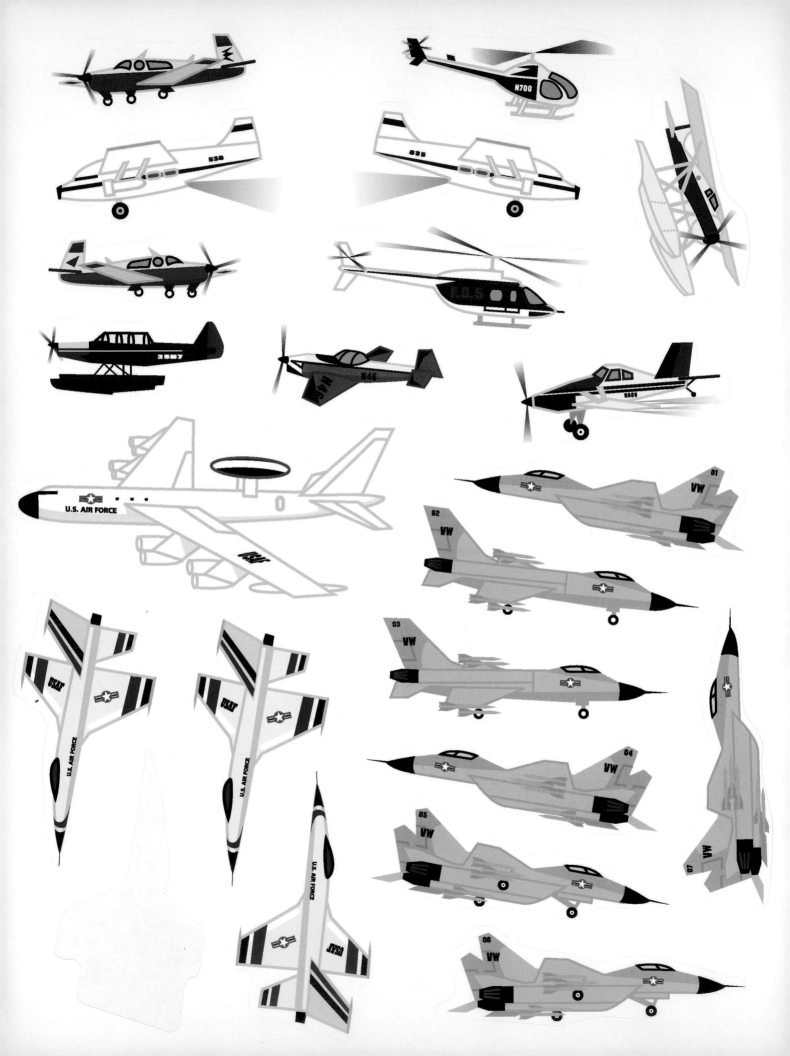

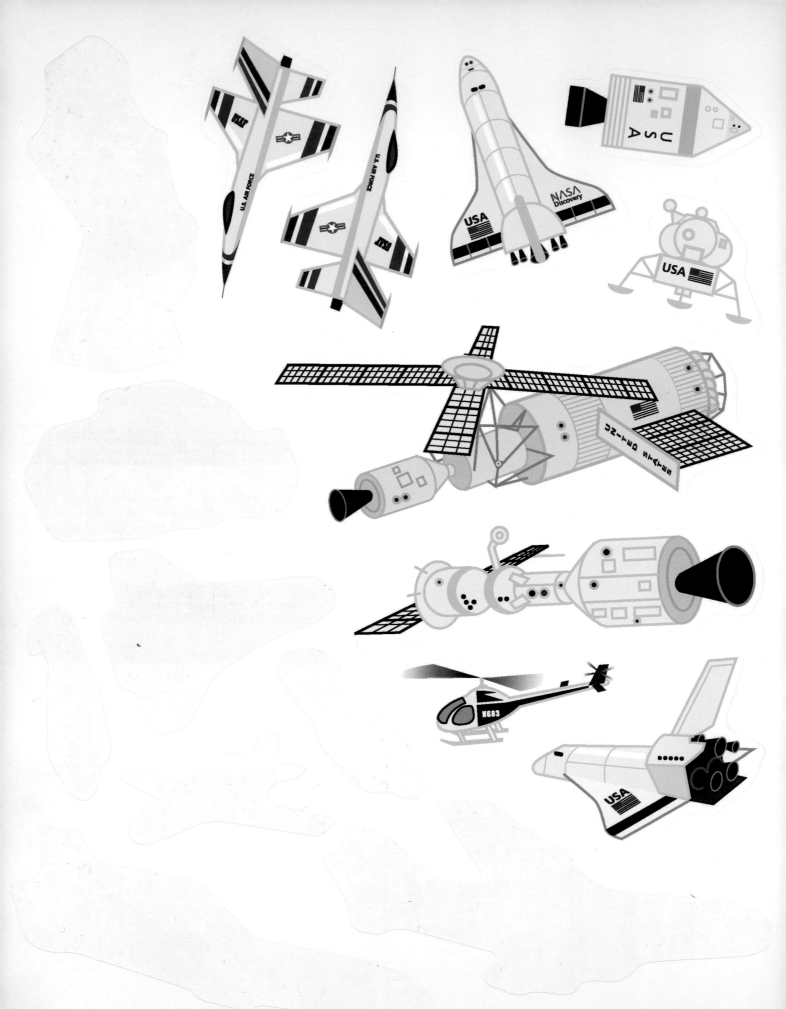

CITY HOSPITAL

Oh no, a forest fire!
It's a good thing we have
special planes to help put it out!

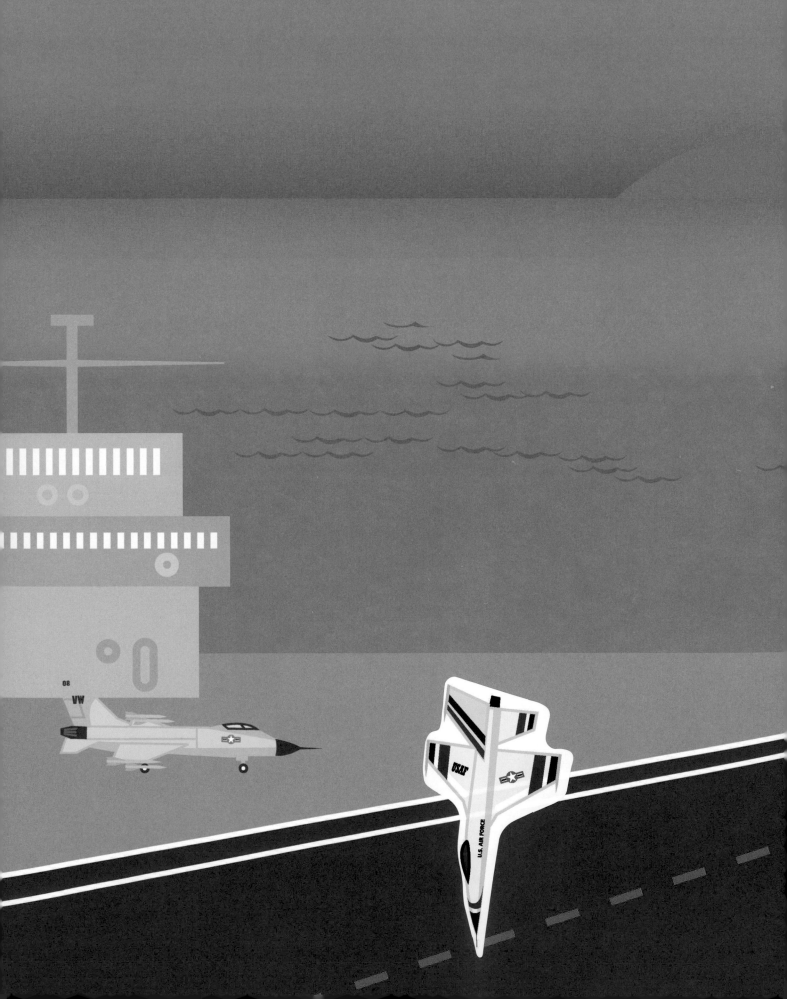

Even speedy military jets
need time to rest.
Help them land on this
aircraft carrier so that
they can refuel.

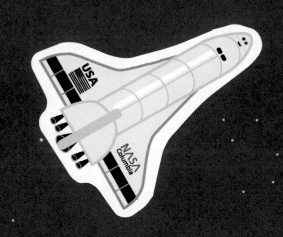

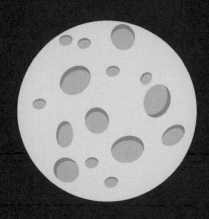

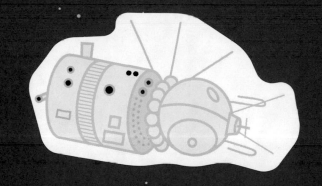

3 – 2 – 1 – blast off!
Spacecraft have helped us explore outer space.

Airplanes fly day and night, taki
people all over the world.